CHARLIE HORSE

Created by Gary Leavitt

Illustrated by Alexandra Sevigny

CHARLIE HORSE

Created by Gary Leavitt

Illustrated by Alexandra Sevigny

Contributing Writers

Jerry Novack

Ed Cameron

Julie Sessa

Patrick Montello

Robert Dawe

Rocky

Paco

Sheena Charlie Lucky Harmonica Clyde

Charlie Horse

Published by Gatekeeper Press

2167 Stringtown Rd, Suite 109

Columbus, OH 43123-2989

www.GatekeeperPress.com

ISBN (hardcover): 9781642375855

eISBN: 9781642375862

Printed in the United States of America

ABOUT THE WRITER, GARY LEAVITT

Gary Leavitt is a popular television and radio personality, as well as a celebrity impressionist and accomplished writer. He has always subscribed to the notions of "standing up for the weak" and "working as a team" to accomplish goals that people may otherwise struggle to do on their own. Gary also believes in leading by example and in never being afraid to learn from others in all aspects of life.

From Gary:

This book is dedicated to my Dad, the greatest writer I have ever read. His strength, wisdom, and love were unmatched.

When his family came to settle down,
Charlie became the new horse in this town.
But whenever Charlie would trot or walk,
some of the horses would whisper and talk.

And then other horses would also make fun
when they saw Charlie Horse trying to run.
But here is something that they did not know,
that this great story will soon come to show.

That it was due to Charlie's bravery
that Charlie Horse received his limp, you see.
Being brave for Charlie Horse
makes him lifelong friends, of course.

Charlie's family moved to a new town,
Hard for some to be the new horse around.
Charlie Horse has a bad limp when he moves
because he has injured one of his hooves.

Despite his limp, Charlie won't be ashamed,
Got it saving a bear cub from the flames!
Charged into the fire, what a close shave!
To pull a cub out — wow, wasn't that brave?

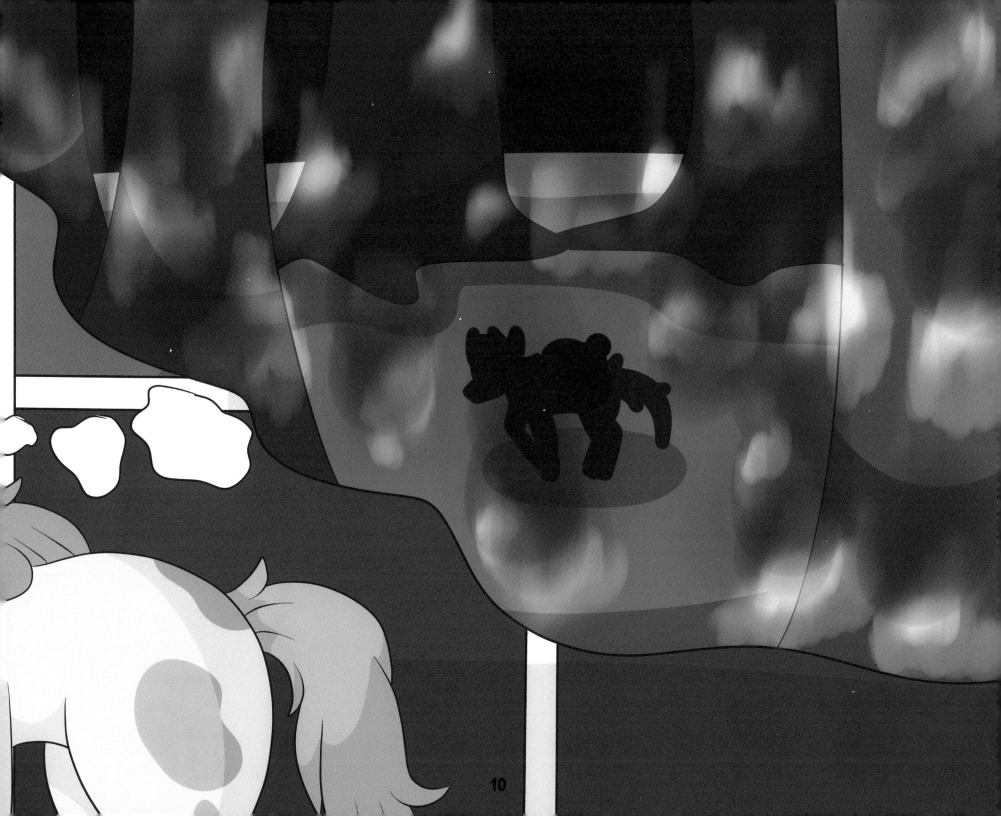

Once Sheena and Clyde asked Charlie to play,
they ran and swam and played all through the day.
Charlie, Sheena, and Clyde horsing around!
Charlie thought, "I really like this new town!"

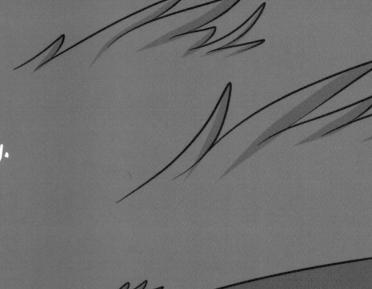

Up and down hills and through pastures they go,
laughing and playing, it was quite a show!
But...lurking near the edges of some big trees,
Clyde can't believe what he hears and he sees.

Some of their friends and really scary things, too.

Clyde said to Charlie, "Now what should we do?"

Now what all of Charlie's friends could not see
is that fate would arrive very shortly.
That Charlie Horse is a friend they will need
because of his ability to lead.

He starts with a limp, breaks into a trot,

Rushes the wolves without even a thought.

The wolves see Charlie and don't seem afraid.

He yells, "Get out, wolves!" but there they all stayed.

What happens next is what really matters.
A roar from the trees as the wolves scatter.

22

A mountain of a bear, Charlie once saved.

You remember the one, in the fire he braved.

The horses felt bad and would all gather round
to thank their friend Charlie, the new horse in town.
Charlie thanked Gary the Grizzly at story's end.
Gary said, "No, Charlie, it's thanks to you, my friend."

(THEME SONG TO BOOK AND
TELEVISION SHOW CHARLIE HORSE)
WRITTEN BY RENEE LEAVITT AND JEFF BATSON
SUNG BY RENEE LEAVITT AND GARY LEAVITT
(THE VOICES OF SHEENA THE SHETLAND
PONY AND GARY THE GRIZZLY)
AVAILABLE TO ORDER ON ITUNES

"FRIENDS FOR LIFE"

EVERY MORNING AS I START MY DAY
I RUN INTO OLD FRIENDS AND I SAY HEY
OLD FRIENDS AND NEW FRIENDS THEY'RE ALL
THE SAME THEY'RE IN MY LIFE TO STAY
WE MIGHT FIGHT BUT WE MAKE IT RIGHT
THEY'LL NEVER GO AWAY
FRIENDS FOR LIFE
THEY'LL BE BY YOUR SIDE
THRU THE YEARS AS THEY FLY
TO LEND A HAND ANYTIME GET YOU BACK ON
TRACK WHEN YOU'RE OUT OF LINE
MAKE YOU LAUGH OR LET YOU CRY CRY CRY
FRIENDS FOR LIFE
DOESN'T MATTER IF WE'RE FAR APART
CAUSE OUR FRIENDSHIP IS A WORK OF ART
WE'LL BE TOGETHER UNTIL THE END BECAUSE
WE'RE IN EACH OTHER'S HEARTS
IN MY WORLD, YOU'RE THE BIGGEST PART
FRIENDS FOR LIFE
THEY'LL BE BY YOUR SIDE
THRU THE YEARS AS THEY FLY
TO LEND A HAND ANYTIME GET YOU BACK ON
TRACK WHEN YOU'RE OUT OF LINE

MAKE YOU LAUGH OR LET YOU CRY
CRY CRY
FRIENDS FOR LIFE
YOU'LL HAVE UPS AND DOWNS
THERE'S NO DOUBT BUT YOU'LL
WORK IT OUT
FRIENDS FOR LIFE
THEY'LL BE BY YOUR SIDE
THRU THE YEARS AS THEY FLY
TO LEND A HAND ANYTIME GET YOU
BACK ON TRACK WHEN YOU'RE OUT
OF LINE
MAKE YOU LAUGH OR LET YOU CRY
CRY CRY
FRIENDS FOR LIFE
THEY'LL BE BY YOUR SIDE
THRU THE YEARS AS THEY FLY
TO LEND A HAND ANYTIME GET YOU
BACK ON TRACK WHEN YOU'RE OUT
OF LINE
MAKE YOU LAUGH OR LET YOU CRY
CRY CRY
FRIENDS FOR LIFE
LA DA LI LI LI
FRIENDS FOR LIFE

27

CPSIA information can be obtained at www.ICGtesting.com
Printed in the USA
BVIW120122250919
559288BV00007B/8